Dear Parents,

Welcome to the Scholastic Reader series. We have taken over 80 years of experience with teachers, parents, and children and put it into a program that is designed to match your child's interests and skills.

Level 1—Short sentences and stories made up of words kids can sound out using their phonics skills and words that are important to remember.

Level 2—Longer sentences and stories with words kids need to know and new "big" words that they will want to know.

Level 3—From sentences to paragraphs to longer stories, these books have large "chunks" of texts and are made up of a rich vocabulary.

Level 4—First chapter books with more words and fewer pictures.

It is important that children learn to read well enough to succeed in school and beyond. Here are ideas for reading this book with your child:

- Look at the book together. Encourage your child to read the title and make a prediction about the story.
- Read the book together. Encourage your child to sound out words when appropriate. When your child struggles, you can help by providing the word.
- Encourage your child to retell the story. This is a great way to check for comprehension.
- Have your child take the fluency test on the last page to check progress.

Scholastic Readers are designed to support your child's efforts to learn how to read at every age and every stage. Enjoy helping your child learn to read and love to read.

—Francie Alexander
Chief Education Officer
Scholastic Education

For Barbara Milagros and Ayanna Josephine,
the fairest of them all
–M.A.T.

For Aunt Mary and Uncle Frank, with love always
–B.L.

Text copyright © 2003 by Scholastic Inc.
Illustrations copyright © 2003 by Barbara Lanza.
All rights reserved. Published by Scholastic Inc.
SCHOLASTIC, CARTWHEEL BOOKS, and associated logos
are trademarks and/or registered trademarks of Scholastic Inc.

Library of Congress Cataloging-in-Publication Data available.

ISBN 0-439-47152-4

12 11 10 9 8 7 6 5 4 3 2   03 04 05 06 07

Printed in the U.S.A. 23 • First printing, May 2003

Snow White

by **Melissa A. Torres**

Illustrated by **Barbara Lanza**

Scholastic Reader — Level 2

SCHOLASTIC INC.

New York Toronto London Auckland Sydney
Mexico City New Delhi Hong Kong Buenos Aires

Snow White was a princess.
She lived long ago.

Everyone but the queen
loved Snow White.

The queen had a magic mirror.
"Mirror, mirror, here I stand.
Who is the fairest in the land?"
the queen asked.

And the mirror said,
"You are fair.
But Snow White is many times
more fair."

The queen was mad!
She told a hunter
to kill Snow White.

But the hunter would not kill her.

"Run away," he said.

"And never come back."

Snow White ran and ran.

She was very tired.

Then she saw a little house.

Snow White peeked inside.

She saw seven little beds.

"I will take a nap," she said.

When Snow White awoke,
she saw seven dwarfs.

The seven dwarfs were kind.
They let Snow White live
in their little house.

The next day, the queen asked,
"Mirror, mirror, here I stand.
Who is the fairest in the land?"

The mirror said, "Snow White, who
lives with the dwarfs, is the fairest."

The queen was very mad!
She thought of an evil plan.
"I will give Snow White a poisoned apple.
She will die.
Then I will be the fairest,"
she said.

The queen dressed up as an old woman.
Then she went to find Snow White.

When the seven dwarfs
went to work,
she knocked on the door.
Knock! Knock! Knock!

Snow White looked out the window.
"I must not open the door
to strangers," she said.
"That's all right," said the queen.
"I don't need to come in.
But I want you to have this apple."

The apple looked so good!
Snow White took it.
After one bite,
she fell to the floor!

The queen's plan worked!
She went home and asked,
"Mirror, mirror, here I stand.
Who is the fairest in the land?"

"You are the fairest," the mirror said.

"At last!" said the queen.

The dwarfs came home.
They found Snow White
on the floor.
They tried to wake her.
But they could not.

The dwarfs placed Snow White
in a glass coffin.
Then they put the coffin
on a hilltop.

One day, a prince
was walking in the forest.
He saw Snow White.
The prince fell in love with her.

The dwarfs let the prince
take Snow White to his castle.
Four boys carried the coffin.
One of them tripped on a rock.
The coffin shook.

The apple popped out of
Snow White's mouth!
She sat up and opened her eyes.

She saw the prince
and fell in love with him.

Snow White and the prince
had a big wedding
and lived happily ever after.

The evil queen was sent far, far away.
And she never hurt anyone again!

Fluency Fun

The words in each list below end in the same sounds.
Read the words in a list.
Read them again.
Read them faster.
Try to read all 15 words in one minute.

blow	**ball**	**day**
grow	**call**	**gray**
show	**fall**	**play**
slow	**tall**	**stay**
snow	**small**	**away**

Look for these words in the story.

lived   **more**   **never**

who   **love**